W9-CKL-008

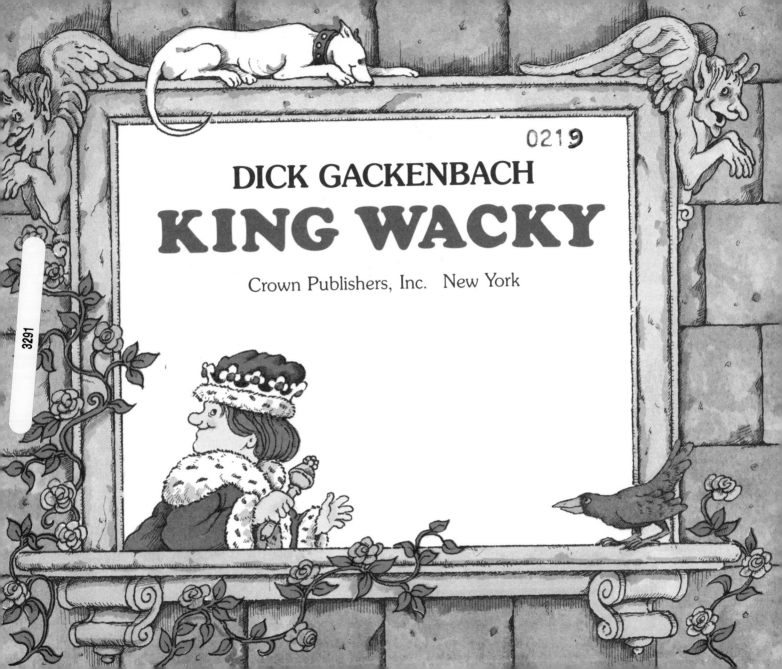

DICK GACKENBACH
KING WACKY

Crown Publishers, Inc.   New York

0219

3291

Copyright © 1984 by Dick Gackenbach. All rights reserved. No part of this publication may be reproduced, stored in a retrieval system, or transmitted, in any form or by any means, electronic, mechanical, photocopying, recording, or otherwise, without prior written permission of the publisher.

Published by Crown Publishers, Inc., One Park Avenue, New York, New York 10016 and simultaneously in Canada by General Publishing Company Limited

Manufactured in the United States of America

Library of Congress Cataloging in Publication Data. Gackenbach, Dick. King Wacky. Summary: Born with his head on backward, King Wacky proceeds to do everything in a backward way. (1. Kings, queens, rulers, etc. — Fiction. 2. Humorous stories) I. Title. PZ7.G117Ki 1984 (E) 83-24044 ISBN 0-517-55265-5

10   9   8   7   6   5   4   3   2   1

To my friend and teacher,
JERRY RETTICH

In the tiny kingdom of Woosey, a baby was born. It was a boy—the son of the king, and a most unusual baby.

"Isn't he beautiful?" said his mother, the queen.

"He is, my dear," replied the king. "But, dear lady, his head is on backward!"

"So it is, dear sir," said the queen. "But, no matter, we will love our son all the more for that."

The good people who lived in Woosey thought the same. "He is our prince," they said, "and we will love him too, no matter which way his head is on."

When Prince Wacky, as the boy was finally named, was old enough to walk, he walked backward.

When the prince began to talk, he spoke in a backward manner as well. Wacky said "goodbye" when he was coming. He said "hello" when he was going. It was "good night" in the morning and "good morning" at night.

In the beginning all this was confusing, but in time it was expected that whatever the prince did, he would do backward. He brushed his teeth before he ate and washed his hands after each meal. When Prince Wacky dined, he sat on the table and his food was placed on a chair.

Over the years, as Prince Wacky grew to be a man, the people of Woosey became truly fond of their backward prince.

"He is kind," they said of him. "Our dear prince has a good heart and is always fair."

So when the day came that Prince Wacky replaced the old king, the people cheered from the bottom of their hearts.

"LONG LIVE KING WACKY," they shouted.

And then, just to please their new king, the people cheered him backward. "WACKY KING LIVE LONG," they cried happily.

Young King Wacky's backward ways made him the most popular king the land of Woosey ever had.

"From now on," King Wacky ordered, "the king will pay taxes to the people." This law made everybody in Woosey very rich.

"Let all the clocks run backward," King Wacky decreed. Because of this law, no one ever complained of being late again.

"Serve the dessert first," King Wacky commanded all the cooks in the land. "And bring the Brussels sprouts last!" From then on, everyone who lived in Woosey always had room in his belly for a good piece of pie.

With Wacky as king everyone agreed it was a joy to live in the land of Woosey.

One day the noble lords of King Wacky's court advised their king: "It is time," they let him know, "for you to have a queen."

"Ah," King Wacky nodded. "That is a bad idea."

The king's reply pleased his noble lords; they knew their king well! When King Wacky said "out," he meant "in." *Up* meant *down; down* meant *up. Good* meant *bad,* and *bad* meant *good.* Therefore, the lords knew King Wacky was willing to seek a queen.

With the king's permission, the lords wrote a message to be sent to mighty King Tub in the nearby land of Bumble.

"In the name of our gracious King Wacky," the message said, "we request the hand of your daughter, Princess Honey, in marriage."

"Perhaps," one lord suggested, "we should add a word or two about King Wacky's unusual ways."

"No, no!" insisted the other lords. "That would never do."

And so, the letter was sealed with the royal seal.

"You will wait for an answer," the lords told the messenger.

Days passed. Finally a tired messenger returned with King Tub's answer. "A splendid idea," King Tub replied. "A marriage would unite Bumble and Woosey. My daughter will arrive to meet your king in seven days."

"Wonderful news!" said the noble lords, "but only seven days to make ready!"

Plans began immediately for the arrival of the future queen.

Bakers baked all sorts and sizes of wedding cakes. Tailors sewed lavish clothes from dawn to sunset. Flags were hung, streets were washed, and houses freshly painted. Schools were closed and peddlers came from everywhere. Woosey was like a giant carnival.

Then, on the seventh day, as promised, Princess Honey arrived at the palace door in her royal carriage. Crowds cheered and danced in the streets as the lovely princess was taken to meet the king.

King Wacky fell in love with the princess the moment he saw her. She was the most beautiful lady King Wacky had ever seen.

Unfortunately, he chose that moment to tell her so.

"Honey," King Wacky said tenderly, "you are the ugliest thing I've ever seen!"

Hearing this, the poor princess burst into a flood of tears. She ran from the palace, home to her father in the land of Bumble.

"King Wacky said I was ugly," Honey sobbed to her father.

Proud King Tub was furious when he heard how King Wacky had ill-treated his dear daughter. In a fit of temper, he made a vow. "I'll have King Wacky's head on a stick," he said.

"Call my generals," King Tub shouted. "March the army to the gates of Woosey," he commanded. "Declare war! Show mercy to no one!"

News of King Tub's marching army traveled fast. Rumors of the coming war spread throughout the land of Woosey.

"It will be a terrible war," everyone agreed. "King Tub's army is a mighty force." The women and children wept and wondered what would become of them. The men of Woosey were sad and thoughtful.

"Perhaps King Wacky will find a way to keep the peace," the people hoped. Everyone gathered at the palace and waited for word from their good king.

Inside the palace, King Wacky and his noble lords were as upset as the people. No one knew what to do. No one wanted war.

"We must tell King Tub that King Wacky meant no harm," suggested a noble lord. "He must understand that when our king says ugly, he means beautiful."

"There is no time for that," said another lord. "King Tub's army is at our very gates."

"Then we must fight," all the lords agreed, "or we will be thought cowards."

So, war it was, and war it would have to be.

"You," King Wacky was told, "will have to tell the people so."

Sadly, King Wacky went out on his balcony and faced the crowd. His subjects were silent and waited anxiously to hear what he had to say.

"I HAVE GOOD NEWS," King Wacky shouted. "WE ARE AT PEACE!"

The people heard no more. Their hearts filled with joy; their cheers reached to heaven. In their great desire for peace, the people had forgotten their king's backward ways. They had forgotten that *good* meant *bad* and that *peace* meant *war.* Had they remembered, they would have hurried home for their weapons and prepared for a cruel war.

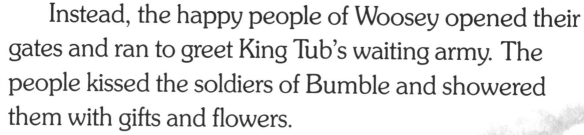

Instead, the happy people of Woosey opened their gates and ran to greet King Tub's waiting army. The people kissed the soldiers of Bumble and showered them with gifts and flowers.

King Tub's generals were surprised and confused.

"What do you think has happened?" asked one general.

"Wacky and Tub must have made up," said another.

The generals and the soldiers returned the kisses to the people of Woosey, tossed away their weapons, and went back home to their families in Bumble.

Now there was time enough to explain everything to King Tub. Once he and Princess Honey understood King Wacky's backward ways, all was forgiven and forgotten.

In due time, there was a grand royal wedding.

"Do you take Princess Honey to be your loving wife?" King Wacky was asked.

"I do not," he answered. But everyone knew he meant he did.

"WACKY KING LIVE LONG!" the people cheered.